W9-BKZ-222

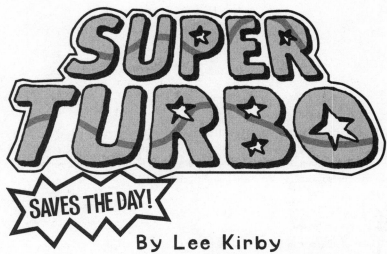

SUPER TURBO

SAVES THE DAY!

By Lee Kirby

Illustrated by George O'Connor

LITTLE SIMON

New York   London   Toronto   Sydney   New Delhi

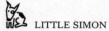 LITTLE SIMON

An imprint of Simon & Schuster Children's Publishing Division • 1230 Avenue of the Americas, New York, New York 10020 • First Little Simon hardcover edition December 2016 • Copyright © 2016 by Simon & Schuster, Inc. All rights reserved, including the right of reproduction in whole or in part in any form. LITTLE SIMON is a registered trademark of Simon & Schuster, Inc., and associated colophon is a trademark of Simon & Schuster, Inc. For information about special discounts for bulk purchases, please contact Simon & Schuster Special Sales at 1-866-506-1949 or business@simonandschuster.com. The Simon & Schuster Speakers Bureau can bring authors to your live event. For more information or to book an event contact the Simon & Schuster Speakers Bureau at 1-866-248-3049 or visit our website at www.simonspeakers.com. Designed by Jay Colvin. The text of this book was set in Little Simon Gazette.

Manufactured in the United States of America 1116 FFG 10 9 8 7 6 5 4 3 2 1

Cataloging-in-Publication Data for this title is available from the Library of Congress.

ISBN 978-1-4814-8885-3 (hc)

ISBN 978-1-4814-8884-6 (pbk)

ISBN 978-1-4814-8886-0 (eBook)

CONTENTS

1

ALL QUIET IN CLASSROOM C

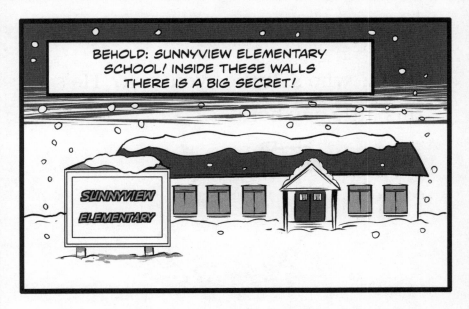

BEHOLD: SUNNYVIEW ELEMENTARY SCHOOL! INSIDE THESE WALLS THERE IS A BIG SECRET!

SUNNYVIEW ELEMENTARY

But for now it was perfectly quiet at Sunnyview Elementary. No kids running down the halls, no teachers giving out pop quizzes, no second-grade students reaching into Turbo's cage—

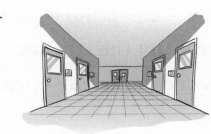

Oh, who's Turbo, you ask? He's this little guy here.

If you couldn't guess, Turbo is a hamster. His fur is mostly white, but he has a big brown spot on his back. He has little pink ears and buck teeth.

And this—er—palace is Turbo's home. Here in the corner of Ms. Beasley's second-grade class.

Turbo, you see, is the official pet of Sunnyview Elementary's Class-room C.

And even on a day like today, when the school was closed for snow, Turbo took his job as class-room pet very seriously.

He made sure to do all his regular classroom pet things.

He drank some water. *GLUG, GLUG, GLUG.*

He ate some pellets. *MUNCH, MUNCH, MUNCH.*

And he ran on his hamster wheel. *SQUEAK, SQUEAK, SQUEAK.*

When he was finished, only a few

minutes had passed. Now what? Usually Turbo liked when the kids went out to recess and he got some peace and quiet. But today it was almost *too* quiet.

Suddenly, it wasn't quiet anymore. Turbo was sure he heard a rustling coming from the cubbies.

Straining his tiny ears, Turbo listened as hard as he could.

"There is definitely something there," Turbo said to no one in particular. "I'm the official pet of Classroom C, and so it is my duty to find out the source of this mystery sound!"

THERE MIGHT BE TROUBLE, SO I SHOULD BE PREPARED. . . .

TURBO MADE HIS WAY ACROSS CLASSROOM C TO THE SOURCE OF THE MYSTERY NOISE. HE WAS SO SNEAKY THAT YOU MIGHT NOT BE ABLE TO SEE HIM. SO HERE'S SOME HELP.

THERE HE IS.

AND HERE.

OVER HERE.

IS THAT?

MAYBE?

Finally, Turbo got to where the noise seemed to be coming from. And then he saw a tail and it belonged to a totally terrible, awful, frightening . . .

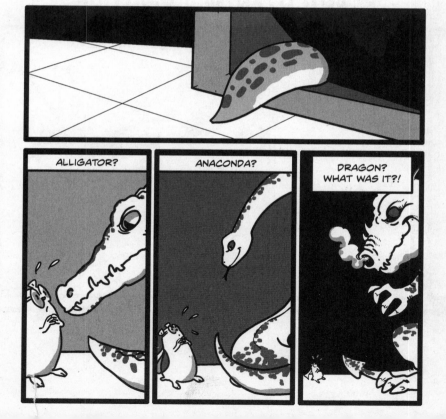

THE MOST TERRIBLE, AWFUL, FRIGHTENING CREATURE

Turbo steadied himself and . . .

"Be careful!" yelled the owner of the tail that surely belonged to the most terrible, awful, frightening creature anyone had ever imagined. "If you grab my tail like that, it might break off!"

The strange new visitor turned

to face Turbo. Now that Turbo could get a good look at him, this stranger wasn't quite the most terrible, awful, frightening creature anyone had ever imagined. Unless the person who imagined him was incredibly afraid of small, green-spotted lizards.

"Who are you?" sputtered Turbo.

"I'm Leo," said the small, green-spotted lizard. "I'm from Classroom A. Who are *you*?"

Gasp! Another classroom pet?!

Turbo had always wondered if there were others like him out

there. Turbo stared suspiciously at Leo. Should he reveal his real name?

"What are you doing here in Classroom C?" Turbo decided to ask first.

"I'm here looking for Angelina," replied Leo. "Have you seen her?"

Turbo rubbed his chin. "I don't think so. What does she look like?"

"Well, she's all fuzzy, just like you. And she's got little pink ears, just like you. And she has buck teeth, just like you. Wait . . . are *you* Angelina?"

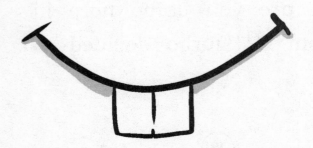

"Of course not! My name is Turbo," said Turbo. *Oh no!* He had accidentally revealed his real name!

"Oh, well," said Leo, "it didn't hurt to ask. All you fuzzy guys look the same to me."

Suddenly another rustling sound came from the reading nook. Turbo closed his eyes and listened while Leo pulled on a mysterious mask.

WITHOUT A WORD, TURBO AND LEO DARTED ACROSS THE CLASSROOM FLOOR. THEY WERE SUPER SNEAKY. SO HERE'S SOME HELP TO SEE THEM.

HERE.

THERE.

PRETTY SURE THIS IS LEO.

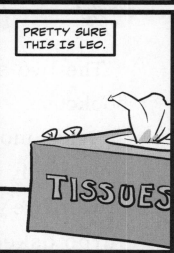

TISSUES

HERE? MAYBE?

THIS IS DEFINITELY TURBO. OR MAYBE A DUST BUNNY. IT'S HARD TO TELL.

The two stopped in front of the bookcase.

"Nice moves!" Leo said. "They were really . . . *super*."

"Uh, are you wearing a mask?" Turbo asked.

"No," said Leo. "Don't be silly."

Turbo wasn't being silly and he was pretty sure he had seen Leo actually run *up* some *walls*.

Then, on the bookcase, a book lurched out several inches from the shelf. A mysterious figure came into view. It was fuzzy. It had pink ears. It had buck teeth.

TURBO GETS A SUPER SURPRISE

"Angelina!" cried Leo as he pulled off his mask.

Ah, so this was Angelina. Turbo wondered what she was doing in Classroom C when she said, "Can you help me get this book? I'm tired of all the books in Classroom B. Too many pictures, not enough words."

Another classroom pet?! Turbo was flabbergasted. What a day today was turning out to be!

Angelina started pushing the book farther toward the edge of the shelf. Quick as lightning, Leo raced up the bookcase to help her.

Meanwhile, Turbo ran off to get a pillow to catch the book.

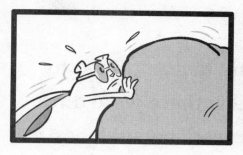

On the count of three, Angelina and Leo gave a big shove, and the book fell right onto the pillow.

Leo skittered down the side of the bookcase, and Angelina simply jumped off the shelf onto the pillow. Now that she was up close, Turbo could see the resemblance.

Turbo shook his head. "I have to admit, I never knew there were any other classroom pets," he said, sort of embarrassed.

"Every classroom has its own pet," explained Angelina. She held out her hand to shake Turbo's.

OUCH!

YEAH, THAT WAS GREAT!

SWEET NEW MANEUVER, GREEN WINGER!

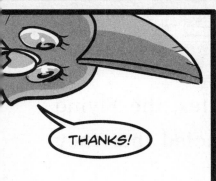

THANKS!

AND, WARREN, MAN, YOU'VE BEEN HOLDING OUT ON US!

DUDE, THOSE SQUIRRELS WERE, LIKE, SO FAST! THAT WAS EASILY OUR BEST BATTLE EVER!

TOTALLY!

After a few minutes, the Flying
Ninja Squirrels signaled that they
were ready.

"We can tell from our battle that
you are honorable opponents," said
Nutkin. "And because we feel we can
trust you, we will tell you what we
are missing. It is the sacred symbol

of our clan, and we believe it gives great strength and speed to its owner. It is . . . the Golden Acorn!"

Super Turbo shot a surprised look at Professor Turtle.

"Weeeell," Professor Turtle said slowly, "I think I know where you can find that."

The Superpet Superhero League and the Flying Ninja Squirrels followed Professor Turtle down the vent to the science lab. Maybe it was because Professor Turtle didn't want to give up the Golden Acorn, or maybe he was just tired after their epic battle, but it was the first time all day that Super Turbo had no trouble keeping up with him.

They exited the vent next to the professor's terrarium. Professor Turtle slowly walked up to the cage and let out a gasp.

8

WHISKERFACE WINS!

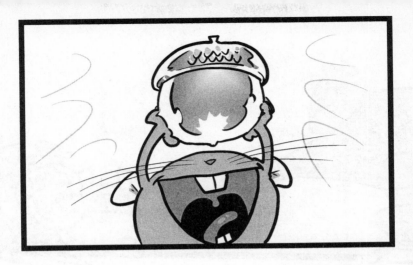

The superpets and Ninja Squirrels stared at the place where the Golden Acorn *should* have been. Suddenly, a familiar and very squeaky voice rang out. "That's right! Your precious Golden Acorn is gone!" said Whisker-face, strolling into view. "I have it!"

"Whiskerface! You rat!" yelled Super Turbo.

"Hey, Nutkin, look! It's the gold-polish salesman!" said one of the Flying Ninja Squirrels. "That's the guy who stole the Golden Acorn!"

"Gold-polish salesman?" asked a Rat Packer in the back.

"Yeah, he asked to see the Golden

Acorn so that he could demonstrate his polish. We showed it to him, and he ran off with it, all the way back to the school," said the other Flying Ninja Squirrel.

"Hey, you told us you defeated the Ninjas in combat . . . ," said another Rat Packer.

"Never mind what the ninny Ninja Squirrels say!" squeaked Whiskerface, his whiskers trembling. "All that matters is that I got the Golden Acorn!"

"And then you *lost* the Golden Acorn," Professor Turtle pointed out.

"Yes, and then I *lost* the Golden Acorn," Whiskerface said through gritted teeth. "But then I *got* the Golden Acorn again! And now that I have it, I will be *unstoppable!*"

"You're nuts!" said Fantastic Fish from within the Turbomobile. "First off, your plan is missing some key steps *again*. Second, do you really believe that acorn is going to give you superpowers?"

"Just ask your new buddies, the Flying Pinhead Squirrels! Or better yet, your old pal Professor Turtle!" Whiskerface squealed.

Super Turbo saw Professor Turtle look sadly down at the ground. Maybe his strength and speed *were* all because of the Acorn. . . .

Suddenly, Super Turbo had an idea. "Yeah, well, that's not what I heard," he said. The Flying Ninja Squirrels, the superpets, and the Rat Packers all looked at him.

"That's not what you heard, huh?" sneered Whiskerface. "Well, why don't you tell me what you heard?"

"Well," said Super Turbo, turning to face Nutkin and her squirrels. "You guys told me how you had to get the Golden Acorn back before it's too late. Before it does any more *damage*. . . ." Super Turbo winked at Nutkin.

"Damage?" squeaked Whisker-face. "What do you mean? What kind of damage?"

Nutkin stepped forward. "It's true that the Golden Acorn gives strength and speed to whoever owns it. But unless you know the secret word to unlock it, the acorn will do the absolute opposite. It will suck out any powers you already have!"

"You're—you're—you're lying!" cried Whiskerface.

Just then, Professor Turtle started to wobble.

SHOOMF!

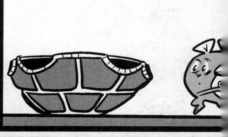

SPROING

The Great Gecko ran up to Professor Turtle. "I can't believe it!" he said. "Professor Turtle has been drained of all his powers!"

"Oh no!" cried the Green Winger. "Who knows what will happen next!"

Whiskerface stared wide-eyed at Professor Turtle.

"You know what?" Whiskerface squeaked. "I don't want this any-way!" He shoved the Golden Acorn into the hands of the Rat Packer next to him and then ran off.

The Rat Packer squeaked in terror and passed the acorn to the rat next

to him. The game of hot potato continued until, finally, one rat handed the Golden Acorn to Super Turbo.

Then all the Rat Packers ran screaming from the lab.

"I believe this belongs to you," said Super Turbo, passing the Golden Acorn to Nutkin.

Nutkin smiled. "I knew we were right to trust you superpets."

"Are . . . they . . . gone . . . yet?" asked Professor Turtle from the floor.

"That was an impressive display of acting!" said Wonder Pig as she and the Great Gecko turned Professor Turtle right-side up.

Professor Turtle answered as slowly as ever.

The superpets and the Flying Ninja Squirrels made their way back to Classroom C. Professor Turtle was really bringing up the rear now, and Super Turbo hung back to walk with him.

"I guess . . . it really was the . . . acorn that . . . made me . . . so fast," Professor Turtle said sadly. "It was nice . . . while it lasted . . . but I guess I'm back . . . to slowpoke Warren."

"But you're not just slowpoke Warren!" Turbo said. "You're a member of the Superpet Superhero League! And whenever you put on your Super Visor, you're never just Warren . . .

o   o   o

Back in Classroom C, the Flying Ninja Squirrels stood in front of the same open window they had snuck in through.

"Superpets," said Nutkin, "the clan of the Flying Ninja Squirrels

will forever be in your debt. You returned our sacred symbol, the Golden Acorn. If you ever need our help, just ask. We live in the big oak tree on the playground."

And with that, the three Flying Ninja Squirrels flew out the window.

"Today was a great day!" said Super Turbo.

"Yeah, it was," said Fantastic Fish.

"We had nachos!" cried Wonder Pig.

"We made a volcano!" exclaimed Boss Bunny.

"We had the best battle ever *and* made some new friends!" said the Great Gecko.

"And I got to be fast . . . for a little while," added Professor Turtle, smiling.

"But, best of all, we defeated evil! Again!" yelled Super Turbo.

HERE'S A SNEAK PEEK AT SUPER TURBO'S NEXT ADVENTURE!

There's a new villain in the classroom. He's big, he's shiny, and he can sharpen a pencil like Super Turbo has never seen. And he stares at Turbo. All. Day. Long. But just when Turbo begins to think that the Pencil Pointer might not be that evil . . . the villain starts spitting pencil shavings! If he keeps at it, Turbo's hamster home will be destroyed. Then Turbo learns that evil isn't only trying to take over his classroom. The rest of the classroom